THE SKY'S THE LIMIT

MANAGING TIME

BY STEPHANIE FINNE

BLUE OWL
BOOKS

TIPS FOR CAREGIVERS

Social and emotional learning (SEL) helps children manage emotions, learn how to feel empathy, create and achieve goals, and make good decisions. Strong lessons and support in SEL will help children establish positive habits in communication, cooperation, and decision-making. By incorporating SEL in early reading, children will be better equipped to build confidence and foster positive peer networks.

BEFORE READING

Talk to the reader about time. Explain that managing time will help him or her reach their goals.

Discuss: How long does it take to do certain tasks? Do you know what should be done first? How do you feel when you are rushed?

AFTER READING

Talk to the reader about creating a schedule. Talk about how a calendar can help with scheduling.

Discuss: What tasks could you add to your calendar? How could you prioritize them?

SEL GOAL

Some students may struggle with time management. Help readers develop time-management skills by reviewing the daily schedule and reminding readers when it is time to move from one project to the next. As time goes on, ask students to help manage the daily schedule for the class.

TABLE OF CONTENTS

CHAPTER 1

WHY MANAGE TIME?

Have you ever been late? Maybe you missed the bus after school because you were catching up with friends. It can be easy to lose track of time. But being **mindful** of time is important. Why?

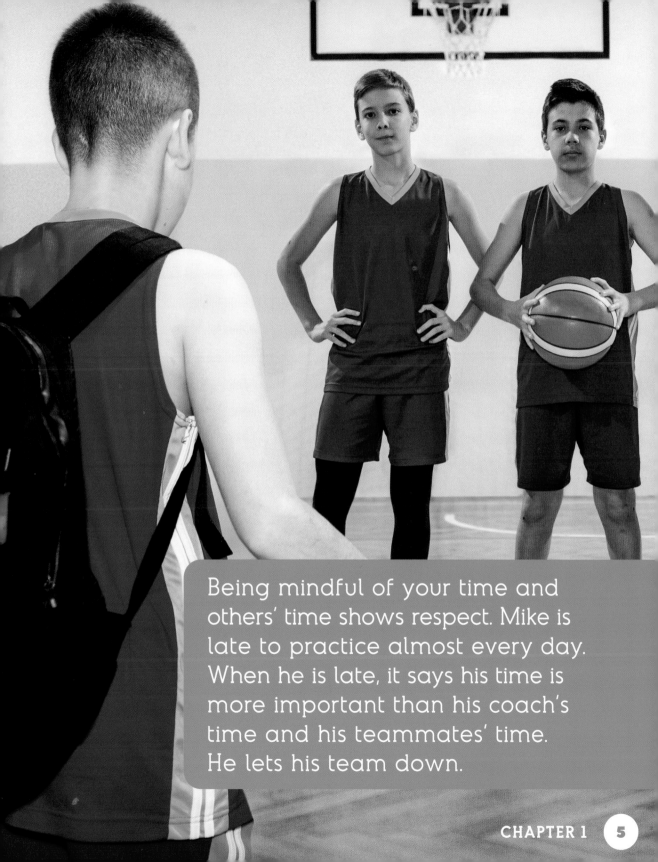

Being mindful of your time and others' time shows respect. Mike is late to practice almost every day. When he is late, it says his time is more important than his coach's time and his teammates' time. He lets his team down.

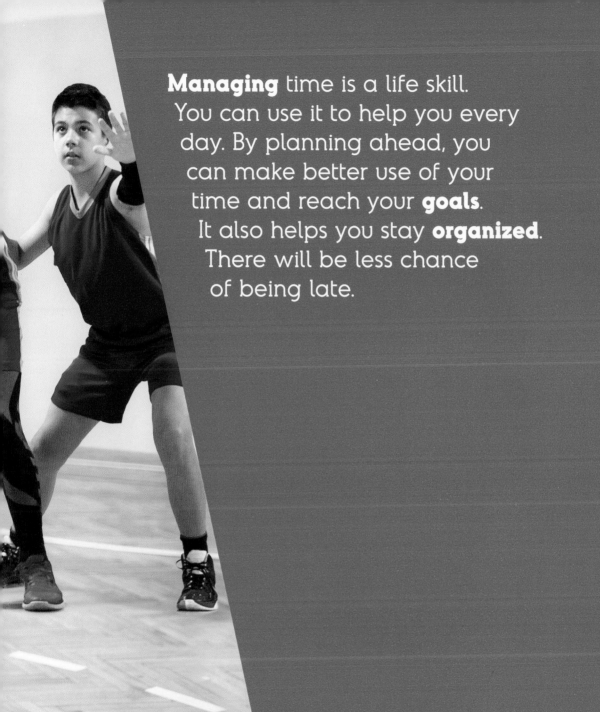

Managing time is a life skill. You can use it to help you every day. By planning ahead, you can make better use of your time and reach your **goals**. It also helps you stay **organized**. There will be less chance of being late.

CHAPTER 2

HOW TO MANAGE TIME

How can you manage your time? Make a plan! Ask an adult for help. Create a **schedule**. Let's say you want to make sure your homework is done on time. You have a project due at school. You want time to play, too.

Make a **visual** schedule.
Block off time for each **task**.

Prioritize your tasks. Decide what needs to be done first. You planned to ride your bike and then do homework. But you ended up riding so long that you didn't have time to finish your homework. You decide that next time you will do homework first.

SCREEN TIME

It is OK to include screen time in your schedule. Set a timer so that you don't lose track of time. Then move on to your next task.

	SUN 13	MON 14	TUE 15	WED 16	THU 17	FRI 18	SAT 19
GMT-05							
7 AM		7:00–7:30 Breakfast					
8 AM		7:30–8:00 Dress & Brush Teeth					
	8–8:30 Breakfast						8–8:30 Breakfast
9 AM		8:30–11:30 School: Reading, Social Studies, Music					
10 AM	10:00–12:00 Chores						10:00–12:00 Basketball Game @ Rec Center Gym
11 AM							
12 PM	12:00–12:15 Shower	11:30–12:00 Recess					
		12:00–12:30 Lunch					12:30–12:45 Shower
1 PM	1:00–1:30 Lunch	12:30–2:40 School: Math, Science, Art			12:30–1:15 Math Test		1:00–1:30 Lunch
2 PM							2:00–4:00 Leo's Birthday Party
3 PM		3:10 Snack					
4 PM		3:30–4:30 Basketball Practice		3:30–4:30 Basketball Practice	3:30–4:30 Flute Lessons		
5 PM		4:45–5:00 Shower					
	5:00–6:00 Dinner						
6 PM	6:00–7:00 Flute Recital	6:00–7:30 Homework	6:00–7:00 Practice Flute	6:00–7:00 Homework			6:00–7:00 Dinner With Grandma
7 PM					7:00–8:00 Study for Math Test		
8 PM	8:00–8:30 Pajamas, Brush Teeth & Read						
9 PM	8:30 Sleep						

Set a goal for each day.
Decide how many math
problems to finish or pages
to read. When is your project
due? Break it into smaller tasks.
Work back from the due date
to schedule them. Then fill in
your schedule. Put each task
in a different color. Now you
have your schedule!

DAILY TASKS

Be sure to include daily tasks
such as getting dressed
and brushing your teeth.
This will help make sure
you have time for everything.

Don't forget to schedule breaks!
Your brain needs time to relax
and have fun in order to reset
and **focus** on the next task.
Getting fresh air, moving
your body, and eating
healthy snacks are all
ways to help your body.

The final step is managing your schedule. Each night, **reflect** on how the day went. In a journal, write five things you are **grateful** for from the day. You can also write down things you didn't have time to do. Once it's on paper, it will be out of your mind and you can get a good night's sleep!

SCHEDULE SLEEP

Make it a **routine** to go to bed and wake up at the same time each day. Getting enough rest will make it easier to manage your time. If you have a hard time falling asleep, talk to a parent or guardian about ways to practice relaxation before bed. This will help your body slow down and sleep.

CHAPTER 3

MANAGING YOUR SCHEDULE

Managing your time will help you feel less **stress**. Making a schedule is just the start. What else can you do? Start a project early! Waiting until the last minute to work on a project can make you feel stressed.

PROJECT SCHEDULE

SUNDAY   RESEARCH ROBOTS AT THE LIBRARY

MONDAY   DECIDE ON TYPE OF ROBOT

TUESDAY   LIST AND GATHER TOOLS AND SUPPLIES

WEDNESDAY   ASSEMBLE AND PROGRAM ROBOT

THURSDAY   TEST ROBOT AND RECORD FINDINGS

FRIDAY   PRESENT AT SCIENCE FAIR

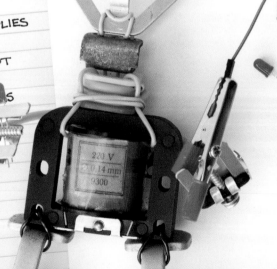

Do one task at a time. This will help you focus all your energy on that task. You will get it done faster and better. This will give you more time to play.

There are many things you want and need to do each day. Managing your time will help you fit them all into your day. How will you manage your time?

GOALS AND TOOLS

GROW WITH GOALS

Time management is a life skill. It takes a lot of practice. Try these goals to help.

Goal: Gather your supplies! Find a calendar or planner that you want to use. Get some colorful highlighters or colored pens.

Goal: Talk through your schedule with a trusted adult. He or she can help you work through your projects. You can discuss priorities and how long things will take.

Goal: Review your schedule every day. Look at what worked and what didn't. Add, move, and adjust as needed.

TRY THIS!

Practice planning. Break your evening into 15-minute chunks. Give each chunk three columns. In the first column, write what you plan to do. In the second column, write what you actually did. In the last column, write about what happened. Reflect on what you did with your time.

GLOSSARY

focus
To concentrate on something.

goals
Things you aim to do.

grateful
Feeling or showing thanks.

managing
Looking after and making
decisions about.

mindful
A mentality achieved by focusing
on the present moment and calmly
recognizing and accepting your
feelings, thoughts, and sensations.

organized
Prepared.

prioritize
To choose the order of tasks so the
most important thing is done first.

reflect
To think carefully or seriously
about something.

routine
A regular sequence of actions
or way of doing things.

schedule
A plan, list of events, or timetable.

stress
Mental or emotional strain, pressure,
or worry.

task
A piece of work that has to be done.

visual
Designed or able to be seen.

TO LEARN MORE

FACT SURFER

Finding more information is as easy as 1, 2, 3.

1. Go to www.factsurfer.com

2. Enter "**managingtime**" into the search box.

3. Choose your book to see a list of websites.

INDEX

Blue Owl Books are published by Jump!, 5357 Penn Avenue South, Minneapolis, MN 55419, www.jumplibrary.com

Copyright © 2021 Jump! International copyright reserved in all countries. No part of this book may be reproduced in any form without written permission from the publisher.

Library of Congress Cataloging-in-Publication Data

Names: Finne, Stephanie, author.
Title: Managing time / by Stephanie Finne.
Description: [Minneapolis]: Jump!, Inc., [2021] | Series: The sky's the limit | Includes index. | Audience: Grades 2–3
Identifiers: LCCN 2020029542 (print) | LCCN 2020029543 (ebook)
ISBN 9781645278559 (hardcover)
ISBN 9781645278566 (paperback)
ISBN 9781645278573 (ebook)
Subjects: LCSH: Time management–Juvenile literature.
Classification: LCC HD69.T54 F56 2021 (print) | LCC HD69.T54 (ebook) | DDC 640/.43–dc23
LC record available at https://lccn.loc.gov/2020029542
LC ebook record available at https://lccn.loc.gov/2020029543

Editor: Jenna Gleisner
Designer: Anna Peterson

Photo Credits: sommthink/Shutterstock, cover; titov dmitriy/Shutterstock, 1 (background); Africa Studio/Shutterstock, 1 (foreground); PrimaStockPhoto/Shutterstock, 3 (left); Vladimir Sukhachev/Shutterstock, 3 (right); Viktoriia Hnatiuk/Shutterstock, 4; domoyega/Getty, 5, 6–7; Shahrul Azman/Shutterstock, 8; Shutterstock, 9, 12–13; Vaclav Volrab/Shutterstock, 10–11; Pekic/iStock, 14–15; Petri Oeschger/iStock, 16–17; AlesiaKan/Shutterstock, 18; Pixel-Shot/Shutterstock, 19; Image Source/iStock, 20–21.

Printed in the United States of America at Corporate Graphics in North Mankato, Minnesota.